Mr. Putter & Tabby
Ring the Bell

CYNTHIA RYLANT

Mr. Putter & Tabby Ring the Bell

Illustrated by

ARTHUR HOWARD

Harcourt Children's Books
Houghton Mifflin Harcourt
Boston   New York   2011

To Steven and Alex and Henry and Dinah
—C.R.

Text copyright © 2011 by Cynthia Rylant
Illustrations copyright © 2011 by Arthur Howard

Harcourt Children's Books is an imprint of
Houghton Mifflin Harcourt Publishing Company.
www.hmhbooks.com

The illustrations in this book were done in pencil, watercolor,
and gouache on 250-gram cotton rag paper.
The text type was set in Berkeley Old Style Book.
The display type was set in Minya Nouvelle, Agenda, and Artcraft.

Library of Congress Cataloging-in-Publication Data

Rylant, Cynthia.
Mr. Putter & Tabby ring the bell / written by Cynthia Rylant ; illustrated by
Arthur Howard.
p. cm.
Summary: While enjoying autumn weather and activities, Mr. Putter,
realizing how much he misses going to school, takes his cat Tabby,
their adventurous neighbor, Mrs. Teaberry,
and her cake-loving dog Zeke to "Show and Tell."
ISBN 978-0-15-205071-9
[1. Old age—Fiction. 2. Neighbors—Fiction. 3. Cats—Fiction. 4. Dogs—
Fiction. 5. Schools—Fiction. 6. Show-and-tell presentations—Fiction. 7.
Autumn—Fiction.] I. Howard, Arthur, ill. II. Title. III. Title: Mr. Putter and
Tabby ring the bell. IV. Title: Mister Putter & Tabby ring the bell.
PZ7.R982Msr 2011
[E]—dc22
2010043403

Manufactured in China
LEO 1 3 5 7 9 10 8 6 4 2
4500295660

1

Crispy Fall

2

The School Bell

3

Mrs. Teaberry

4

Pet Tricks

5

Show-and-Tell

6

The Worst Ever!

1

Crispy Fall

It was fall.

Mr. Putter and his fine cat, Tabby,
loved fall.

Mr. Putter liked the apples.

Tabby liked the leaves.

They both liked the crispy wind.

And sometimes their neighbor,
Mrs. Teaberry, brought them
rhubarb trifle.
They *really* liked that.
Fall was fun.

2

The School Bell

One day while Mr. Putter
was raking leaves
and Tabby was attacking leaves,
they heard the school bell ring.
Dong. Dong. Dong.
Mr. Putter stopped raking.
He looked at Tabby.
"I miss school," said Mr. Putter.
"I miss pencils and books."

Tabby stopped attacking.
She purred.
"I miss globes and erasers,"
said Mr. Putter.

Dong, dong, dong went the bell.
"I would like to go back
to school," said Mr. Putter,
"for just one day."

Just then, Mrs. Teaberry's good dog,
Zeke, ran by.
Zeke was wearing half a cake
on his head.
(The other half was inside Zeke.)

Mr. Putter looked at Zeke.

Mr. Putter looked at Tabby.

"I have an idea," said Mr. Putter.

Tabby purred and purred.

She loved Mr. Putter's ideas.

3

Mrs. Teaberry

Mr. Putter knocked on
Mrs. Teaberry's door.
Zeke stood beside Tabby.
(All of the cake was now
inside Zeke.)

Mrs. Teaberry opened the door.

"There you are!" she said.

"Yes, here I am," said Mr. Putter.

"No, I meant Zeke," said Mrs. Teaberry.

"He stole the banana cake!"

"That was banana cake?" asked Mr. Putter.

Mr. Putter looked sad.

"I love banana cake," he said.

"So does Zeke," said Mrs. Teaberry.

Everyone looked at Zeke.

Zeke looked happy.

Zeke looked fun.

Zeke looked *showy*.

"Mrs. Teaberry," said Mr. Putter,

"I have an idea."

"Oh, good!" said Mrs. Teaberry.
"I love ideas!"
"Do you love globes and erasers?"
asked Mr. Putter.
"Pardon me?" said Mrs. Teaberry.
Mr. Putter began telling her his idea.
Tabby purred and purred.

4

Pet Tricks

The first grade teacher
at the school
thought it was a lovely idea.
"Show-and-tell?" she said
to Mrs. Teaberry on the phone.
"What a good idea! The children
love cats and dogs. Do yours
do tricks?"

Mrs. Teaberry looked at Zeke.

He was wearing his water bowl.

"Sort of," said Mrs. Teaberry.

"Wonderful!" said the teacher.

"Come right over!"

Mrs. Teaberry called Mr. Putter.

"It worked," she said.

"We're going to school."

"Hooray!" said Mr. Putter.

"But the teacher wants
pet tricks," said Mrs. Teaberry.

"Pet tricks?" asked Mr. Putter.
He looked at Tabby,
who was napping in the soup pot.
"Uh-oh," said Mr. Putter.
Tabby knew how to nap.
Tabby knew how to purr.
But could Tabby do tricks?

5

Show-and-Tell

Mr. Putter and Tabby
and Mrs. Teaberry and Zeke
walked to the school.
They stepped through the door.
"It smells just like school,"
said Mr. Putter.

They found the first grade room.

Mrs. Teaberry straightened
Zeke's tie.

Mr. Putter patted Tabby's head.

Then they went in.

Mr. Putter was in heaven.

It was a room filled with
books and pencils and globes
and erasers and—best of all—
children!

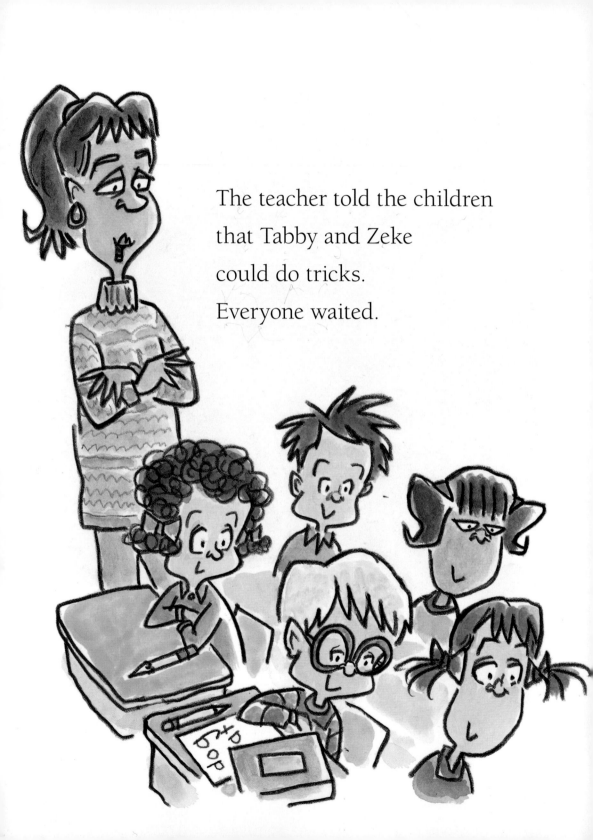

The teacher told the children
that Tabby and Zeke
could do tricks.
Everyone waited.

Tabby purred.

Zeke scratched at his tie.

No one did a trick.

"Uh-oh," said Mr. Putter.

"Oh, dear," said Mrs. Teaberry.

Suddenly the school bell
began to ring.
DONG!
It was very loud!
Tabby jumped straight up in the air!
She landed on a little girl's
lap in the front row.
The little girl screamed.

DONG!

Zeke jumped straight up in the air!

He landed in a box of cupcakes.

"Don't eat all the cupcakes!"

the teacher yelled.

DONG!

Zeke ate all the cupcakes.

Then Zeke did a trick.

It was a good trick.

Tabby did it, too.

It was a *disappearing* trick!

And that was the end
of show-and-tell.

6

The Worst Ever!

Back home, Mr. Putter
made tea for Mrs. Teaberry
while Tabby and Zeke napped.
They looked at Zeke.
His tie was full of cupcake.
They looked at Tabby.
Her tail was quite festive.

Mr. Putter smiled.

Mrs. Teaberry smiled.

Then they started laughing.

It had been the worst show-and-tell ever!

But they were happy.

Mr. Putter got to go to school.

And Tabby and Zeke learned

a few new tricks!